Artie's sister, Edith

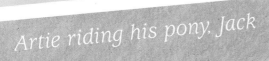

Artie riding his pony, Jack

Artie on his pony

Clarence, the pilot who let Artie fly with him

When Artie Was Little

by Harriet Berg Schwartz

pictures by Thomas B. Allen

Alfred A. Knopf ⋇ New York

THIS IS A BORZOI BOOK PUBLISHED BY ALFRED A. KNOPF, INC.

Library of Congress Cataloging-in-Publication Data
Schwartz, Harriet Berg
When Artie was little / by Harriet Berg Schwartz ; illustrated by Thomas B. Allen
p. cm.
Summary: Now an old man, Artie enjoys sitting on his front porch and telling the neighborhood children
about his pony Jack, his dog Skipper, and his trip with a barnstormer when he was a boy.
ISBN 0-679-83236-X (trade) — ISBN 0-679-93236-4 (lib. bdg.)
[1. Old age—Fiction.] I. Allen, Thomas B., ill. II. Title.
PZ7.S40765Wh 1996
[E]—dc20 94-33351

Manufactured in Singapore

10 9 8 7 6 5 4 3 2 1

---

*To Aram and Molly, Ian and Gwen—may they remember their
childhoods with the joy that Art Gulick remembers his*
—H. B. S.

To the family of Albert V. Truglio, a lifelong resident of Hoboken
(1920–1992)
— T. B. A.

When Artie was a little boy, his hair was white and his eyes were blue and his cheeks were pinky red. The cars were high and square and broke down all the time. People came from all over to have Artie's father repair them.

When Artie was little, his mother sold food at a stand across the road from the garage. She baked pies and muffins and fried up potato chips. She sold hamburgers and hot dogs with homemade sauerkraut and homemade mustard. People came from all over to buy Mrs. Kramer's food.

When Artie was an old man, a little girl asked, "Artie, what was the best food you ever ate?" Artie told her about his mother's homemade apple pie and potato chips sold at the roadside stand.

When Artie was little, he woke up one Christmas morning and found a beautiful brownish gray pony tied to the tree right there inside his house.

"Dad," said Artie, "his ears are very big. Are you sure it's a pony?"

"Of course it's a pony!"

"I think it's a donkey. You told me I was too little to have a pony."

"It's a pony all right," his father insisted.

"Then I'll call him Jack." Artie stroked Jack's velvety soft nose and rough sides. "I'll take good care of him, Dad. Thanks." Artie kept Jack's stall clean, fed him oats, and combed him every day.

When Artie was an old man, a little boy asked, "Artie, what was the best Christmas present you ever got?" Artie told him about his pony, Jack, and how he thought he was a donkey.

When Artie was little, he was out riding Jack when he met a man on a beautiful brown stallion. The man wore yellow gloves, shiny boots, and a derby hat. "Ride along with me and keep me company," said the stranger from high up on his horse. And Artie did.

"I want high boots and yellow gloves for riding," Artie announced that evening at supper.

"Certainly not," said his father.

"The idea!" agreed his mother. "A child in yellow gloves!"

Artie brought his new friend home. He wanted to show his mother and father the handsome man on the beautiful horse who wore yellow gloves, shiny boots, and a derby hat.

"My goodness gracious," exclaimed Mrs. Kramer after the stranger rode away. "Do you have any idea who you've been riding with? That's the Mayor of Hoboken!"

When Artie was an old man, a little girl asked, "Artie, who was the most famous person you ever met?" Artie told her how he'd ridden beside the Mayor of Hoboken.

When Artie was little, his sister, Edith, died.

Artie's father closed the garage for two weeks and just sat in his big chair near the fireplace. Artie, his aunt Hedwig, and his mother, who couldn't stop crying, went to a department store to pick out a dress for Edith to be buried in.

"Anna, which dress do you think is best?" asked Artie's aunt.

"Oh, I don't know. Ask Artie which one he likes."

Artie's nose was pressed against the glass display case. He pointed to a pink dress with a white sash. The dress Artie chose was the one they put on little Edith. Then they had the funeral. Artie missed his sister for a long time.

When Artie was an old man, a little boy asked, "Artie, do you have any brothers or sisters?" Artie told him about his little sister, Edith, and how he'd picked out her dress when she died so many years ago.

When Artie was little, his mother cooked a nice beef stew for Sunday dinner.

"What's this stuff?" he said, screwing up his nose.

"A scrumptious beef stew," answered Artie's mother. "You'll love it."

"Simply delicious!" exclaimed Aunt Hedwig.

"Eat it!" commanded Artie's father.

"It's full of vegetables," said Artie. "I don't want any." He just stared at his plate.

Finally, his mother said, "All right. Take it out to Skipper. He'll like it fine."

Artie crossed the yard and put the plate down in front of his dog. He watched as Skipper began eagerly lapping it up. He seemed to be enjoying it so much that Artie decided to kneel right down and taste some himself. Skipper didn't growl. He just shifted aside to make room for Artie. Artie reached into the dish for a potato. "Mmm. Not bad," he thought. Then he lapped up a carrot. Next he tried a chunk of meat. "Stew is pretty good," he said to himself. Skipper finished the gravy.

When Artie was an old man, a little girl asked him, "Artie, who was your best friend when you were little?" Artie told her that his very best friend was his dog, Skipper, because he knew how to share.

When Artie was little, he saw an amazing sight. Airplanes were parked along the edge of a huge field near his house. Others were landing and taking off, and some men were standing around.

"Do you guys fly planes? Wow!" shouted Artie.

"We're barnstormers, kid."

"What are 'barnstormers'?"

"People pay to see us do trick flying. If you tell everyone you know that we're here, you can come and watch all you want for free."

Soon the whole neighborhood knew about the barnstormers.

The next Saturday morning a lot of people came to the airfield. The planes took off, one after the other, as the crowd shouted with wonder and excitement.

"My goodness, did you see that?" A plane was rolling over and over.

"Oh, no, he's going to crash! Isn't it incredible? Isn't it amazing?" Another plane had climbed high in the sky and was diving toward the ground. It swooped back up at the very last moment.

"He'll fall! He'll fall! How can they do it?" Two men stood between the wings of a biplane while it banked in a wide circle above the field.

Artie thought, "Flying must be the greatest thing in the world! When I grow up, I'm going to be a pilot."

"Clarence, take me for a ride in your plane, please," Artie begged the pilot.

"Well, I don't know about that," answered Clarence. "You're sort of little."

"Please, please. I'm not scared! My parents won't mind, I know it!" Artie pulled at the pilot's sleeve.

So Clarence strapped Artie into the front seat of the plane, then climbed into the cockpit behind him. The plane shivered and shook as it raced down the field. Suddenly, they were in the air.

"There's my house! There's the barn! There's Mom by the food stand! There's the garage!" Far below and as tiny as pictures in a book, Artie saw his school and the woods where he rode with the Mayor of Hoboken. He could see the road that passed by the garage. "Someday, I really am going to be a pilot," he said.

And when he grew up, he was.

When Artie was an old man, a little girl asked, "Artie, what was the most exciting day of your life?" Artie told her about the day a pilot named Clarence took him for a ride in his plane.

When Artie was an old man, his hair was white and his eyes were blue and his cheeks were pinky red. He liked to sit on his front porch and watch the cars zooming by and talk to the neighborhood children. He thought about his pony, Jack. He thought about his best friend, Skipper, who knew how to share, and about the first time he tasted beef stew. His mouth watered as he remembered his mother's homemade potato chips and mustard. He liked to remember his little sister, Edith, and that he had picked out the dress for her burial. He liked to remember the Mayor of Hoboken.

And more than anything else, he liked to think of the day he flew in Clarence's biplane and saw the world from the air for the very first time.

Artie and a barnstormer

Artie with his bull calf

Artie on his tricycle

Artie and his mother (sitting) with his aunt and cousin